FOOD OF TH

To/Adrian

I hope you like the
taste of Food Of the Gods
(almost as nice as No.8k Cake!)

EM DEHANEY

Food Of The Gods 2

ISBN-13: 978-1983960376

ISBN-10: 1983960373

Cover artwork by Matthew Cash

Food Of The Gods 4

Food Of The Gods 6

INTRODUCTION

Most of the stories in this collection have been published elsewhere in one form or another, and I am hugely grateful to every editor who has chosen my work out of the pile, taken the time to read it, consider it, make notes on it and suggest ways to improve it. No good book is the product of one single person. Being a writer means treading a line of insular artistic solitude and collaborative compromise. As the great Stephen King once said, 'Write with the door closed, edit with the door open.'

With that in mind, there are a few people and publications I would like to thank (in no particular order):

The British Fantasy Society, who included the titular story for this anthology, Food Of The Gods, in their BFS Horizons Issue 4.

The 84 Words writing group, especially Adrian Flaherty (without whom the group would not exist), Peter Germany, Sally Skeptic and Matt Hill. I dabble in poetry from time to time, I do not claim to be a poet. To a real poet my poetry is, I'm sure, awful. But dabble I do, and the poem in this collection, Under The Fringe Tree, was a result of one of the writing prompts from 84 Words. They are a wonderful bunch, and the combination of writing, tea and cake makes No.84 Tearoom in Gravesend one of my favourite places to be.

Elizabeth Haynes, for providing me with the inspiration to just get on and WRITE, for being generally lovely, and for introducing me to The Kent NaNo Group. National Novel Writing Month (NaNoWriMo for short-ish) is one of those things that sounds crazy when you say it out loud: write a 50k novel in 30 days? Why of course! I'm sad to say I've never managed the full 50'000 words yet, but who knows, maybe one day…

Rosemary Long of Tribe Media, who first published The Disappearing Mermaid in the Thief literary journal.

Siren's Call Publications for publishing Bellarmine (one of my very early short stories) and The Story of Moses (my love letter to Lovecraft) in their Women In Horror e-zine.

Christine Morgan of Fossil Lake, who puts out epic anthologies with titles such as Unicornado and Sharkasaurus. Christine gave me my first paid writing gig, for the story The Mermaid's Purse, although I did the cheesily predictable thing of not cashing the cheque and saving it to put in a frame.

All the fantastic writers I have met online and in real life over the past couple of years, particularly in the horror community. Contrary to popular belief, horror writers are not a melancholy bunch of weirdos hunched in the dark, drinking too much. They are a funny as fuck bunch of weirdos, some hunched, some not. I couldn't possibly comment on the drinking.

Matty-Bob Cash, The Reverend Burdizzo to my Black Nun and partner in crime at Burdizzo Books. The first to say 'YES' to one of my early submissions and a constant support in the whole writing game. This book wouldn't exist without you. Mainly because you designed the amazing cover, but still, fanks a million and all that.

Chris, for giving me time and space to realise my lifelong dream of being a writer and bringing me cups of tea when I'm holed up with my laptop.

And finally, thank YOU for buying this book, my first and hopefully not my last.

Em Dehaney, January 2018

Food of the Gods

It was not long after he returned from Venezuela that the dreams began. The three-week tasting tour had brought Alderney Finch to the brink of bankruptcy, but only the finest ingredients were good enough for House of Finch. He rather grandly named his chocolate shop House of Finch, when in reality it was a cramped two-up two-down in a dowdy area of London yet to become fashionable.

On the day in question, while working on a new batch of strawberry and balsamic vinegar truffles in his tiny backroom kitchen, the razorblade Alderney was using to cut slivers of freeze-dried fruit slipped and the tip of his index finger popped off with a crunch. Blood spurted from his ruined digit with such ferocity that a scarlet mist appeared on the opposite wall of the kitchen. He stood transfixed by the colour of his own life pumping onto white marble. Sharp pain flooded in, snapping him out of his stupor. He staggered out of the kitchen, through the small shop front and flagged down a taxi. The tinkle of the bell over the shop door was still ringing in his ears when he got to Accident & Emergency.

After a six and a half hour wait with his hand held in the air to stop himself bleeding to death, he was stitched up and sent home. The nurse berated him for not bringing the end of his finger. Of course, Alderney thought to himself, the first thing I wanted to do when I was spraying blood in every direction was get down on my hands and knees to look for the foreskin of my now circumcised finger. Idiot woman.

When the taxi dropped him back outside the shop he checked his watch, but the smears of blood on its face made him feel wobbly. Alderney decided to go to bed and worry about cleaning up in the morning. As he stumbled through the kitchen in the dark, he grabbed a handful of lime and basil bonbons to nibble while he climbed the stairs to his flat. He popped the first sweet into his mouth. The burst of flavour on his tongue was so intense it was touching orgasmic. The white chocolate shell provided a smooth vanilla capsule for the violent citrus cream, which exploded onto his taste buds at the optimum melting point. The basil note was dense and damp like a rainforest, and lingered gently once the initial hit of the lime had faded. In all his twenty-three years as a chocolatier, Alderney Finch had never tasted anything so heavenly. He crammed the other four bonbons into his mouth at once, wanting to drown in the ecstasy of his creation.

By the time he reached the landing they were all gone. He considered running back down the stairs and shoving his face in the tray, guzzling the remaining chocolates like a pig at the trough, but fatigue got the better of him and he let himself into the cramped flat, took off his blood encrusted whites and lay down on the bed. The throbbing in his finger was on the edge of unbearable, and if he didn't sleep now he would be up all night with the pain.

...the shadow serpent slowly inched its way up the side of the pyramid. Slithering over each step, the snake made its sinister progress to the top. Soon the sun would be gone, and the shadow would be made flesh. A low rumble reverberated through the stone, louder and louder until it became a thunderous roar. A thousand voices chanting together. Chanting the name...

Alderney awoke damp with cold sweat and a deep ache in his bones. His whole hand pulsed angrily and he was sure the cut was infected. But it was Saturday, the busiest day for his little artisan chocolate shop, and he couldn't afford a day off. He heaved himself off the bed, peeled the t-shirt from his clammy back, put on a clean set of whites and padded downstairs to open up.

The scene that greeted him was more charnel house than chocolate box. Blood stained the ceiling and dribbled down the wall tiles. Blood congealed on the floor and streaks of blood decorated the strip lights. Blood encrusted the frosted glass window and blood pooled in his stainless steel mixing bowls. A thick puddle of the stuff had coagulated on his marble tempering slab in what looked like of a map of South America. And worst of all, there was a fine blood spatter decorating the tray of lime and basil bonbons he scoffed down in the dark last night.

But they *were* delicious.

He plucked one of the small, white chocolate domes and held it up for inspection. His blood had fallen onto the shiny surface in a uniform fleckle he could not have recreated with his airbrush if he tried. The overall effect was certainly pleasing on the eye, like an inverted fly agaric toadstool. His saliva glands anticipated the sharp, mossy sweetness of the filling.

Into his mouth it went. It was good. Even better than he remembered.

The unfinished strawberry and balsamic truffles sat next to the tray of lime and basil bonbons. His blood had settled on the surface of the dark paste, giving it the look of black suede. Alderney glanced at the clock. He only had half an hour until the shop was due to open. No time to make any more batches today. He dusted the truffles with cocoa powder and carried both trays through to the glass display counter.

Business was brisk, and the strictly controlled air-conditioning in the shop cooled the fever brewing inside Alderney. He had a twang of guilt the first time someone asked for the lime and basil. But he had bills to pay and he knew they were the most delicious chocolates he had ever crafted. In a quiet period he snaffled one of the strawberry and balsamic truffles.

It was a sensory feast.

The mouthfeel was exquisite. Fresh strawberry fizzed like pure summer on his tongue, then the curious, dark acidity of the balsamic came through. Alderney couldn't believe the miniscule amount of blood on the chocolates had done this, and throughout the day managed to convince himself it was his talent as a chocolate artiste, his flair for flavour combinations and his search for the finest ingredients that had brought forth such divine creations.

…the figure on top of the pyramid cast a long shadow. The air was dense and sticky, and steam rose from the crowd

below. All around was the constant drone of chanting. The same word over and over and over. The serpent knew the moment was at hand. He was being called. Soon he would take his rightful place above the masses. Soon they would show their devotion. They would give freely, and he would take hungrily. Their warm, lifeblood would fill his belly. It would pour down the steps of the pyramid, bathing his followers in a sea of red. They would writhe in an orgy of bloodlust…

When Alderney woke on Sunday, the smell of copper filled his nostrils. Blood soaked his pillow and the dressing hung limply from his oozing hand. No time to go back to the hospital though, he had work to do. Recipes had been pinging around in his mind since yesterday and now he had all day to make them a reality. Rosehip and mint fondant, pandan leaves with a sprinkle of curry powder, *gianduja* spiked with English mustard, pine resin toffee, crispy wafers of parmesan cheese coated with coffee granules, sugar crystals infused with lemon and seaweed. And all enrobed in the darkest, sexiest, silkiest chocolate made with rare *criollo* beans grown on the shores of Lake Maracaibo. He worked all day and night, tempering, mixing and tasting. The sodden bandage soon fell from his hand and although he felt the slow drip, drip, drip down his wrist, he ignored it. Falling into bed as the birds were breaking into their morning song, Alderney was convinced he had made the finest cacao confections the world had ever known.

... the priest stood, his face shrouded in darkness. The outline of his feathered golden headdress was black against the purple sky. He awaited the kiss of the serpent's tongue with arms outstretched and chest bared. A thick crack of lightning lit the

gloom. The priest's eyes flashed red. His tongue flicked out between his lips, testing the air. From his mouth came one word. The name, the spirit, the snake, the god, the divine, life, sex, food, death. One word...

'Quetzalcoatl!' shouted Alderney, waking himself up with a jolt. The strange gibberish faded from his mind as he scrabbled to remember the name of the girl lying next to him. Katie? Claire? Christina? Kelly. Yes, Kelly. Or was it Kerry?

Alderney had been celebrating. His week had been nothing short of amazing. Every batch of the new flavours sold out within hours and the social-media buzz around his shop was going crazy. He had been given a five-truffle review in The Chocolate Bible and The Chocolatier wanted to interview him for their next issue. On Saturday the last remaining creations sold by midday, so he had gone out, got far too drunk and had to be escorted home by the fine young lady who now lay in his bed, drooling on the pillow. As if on cue, she opened her eyes.

'Morning.'

'Morning…err…'

'Keeley. My name's Keeley. Don't worry, I can't remember yours either. But this was fun. Let me know if you wanna hook up again some time. I'll leave you my number.' She gathered up her clothes and left the bedroom, struggling to squeeze past the sacks of cacao beans crowding the hallway.

Despite his pounding head, Alderney needed to get his next collection of chocolate concoctions underway. The London Confectionary Awards were in a few weeks, and House of Finch was a late entry in six categories. His finger was healing nicely, and once he had taken a couple of paracetamol for his headache, he set to work on a *bouchon* filled with parsnip and champagne cream. But no matter how hard he tried, the chocolate for the cork-shaped shell would not temper. In frustration, he gave up the tempering and started working on the flavour infusions, but the cream kept curdling and the caramelised parsnips were burned, giving an acrid, bitter taste. After throwing his fourth attempt in the bin, Alderney felt the excesses of the previous night catching up with him. Unable to keep his eyes open, he slumped in the corner of the kitchen, falling asleep within seconds.

...the priest's red eyes were alive with the spirit of the shadow serpent. His body was merely a vessel now, filled with an unrelenting hunger.

'You know what you must do,' the priest spoke as he raised his hands above his head. The obsidian shard flashed as he brought it down in an arc onto the naked chest laid bare on the altar. The sharpened edge pierced through flesh. The crowd let out screams of exaltation. As the blood spilled out and ran down the steps, so the crowd rushed forward to dance in the divine rain.

'Quetzalcoatl is hungry. Feed him. Feed him. Feed…'

'…him,' Alderney murmured as he stirred.

Staring at the abandoned trays of mistakes and abominations strewn around the kitchen, he knew what he had to do. Stroking his raw fingertip, he reached for the razor blade.

House of Finch swept the board at The London Confectionary Awards, and Alderney was the new shining star of the chocolate world. Countless interviews and photo shoots followed. A newspaper column, a recipe book and even a television show were all on the cards and he hired an agent to keep on top of everything. He ended his lease on the shop, moved out of the miniature flat and into a penthouse apartment overlooking the river. He lost count of how many times he explained away his bandaged hands to journalists and daytime television presenters with anecdotes of his clumsy kitchen antics. A knife slippage here, a scalding hot pan there. But soon, the dreams returned.

...the priest plunged his arm deep into the chest cavity and wrenched out the still pulsating heart of the girl prone on the altar. Her face was a mask of agony. The priest leered gleefully over the body as he raised the organ to his mouth.

'Quetzalcoatl is hungry.'

The priest's tongue flickered out to caress the heart. Its two prongs shivered in separate anticipation of the feast...

He found Keeley's number on a folded receipt in his wallet. She had underlined her name three times, so he wouldn't forget. They met at a bar. Alderney asked her if she wanted to see a chocolate factory. She made a joke about his Willy Wonka, and they set off. Alderney had been either blind drunk or foggily hungover the last time he was with Keeley. As he followed her down the steps of the tube station, he realised how young she was. She talked non-stop about soap operas, her friends, college, the new summer blockbuster she had just seen at the cinema, whether her cat was pregnant and if so what she would call the kittens. When they reached his new workshop, he was almost looking forward to what he had to do, just to shut her up.

Alderney flicked on the lights at the bank of switches by the door, and the girl let out a gasp. The room was more like a laboratory than a kitchen, with two long white benches stretching the length of the slim space. There were copper kettles, freeze driers, juicers, blenders and a huge condensing unit with glass bulbs that hung down like fruit. Two metal canisters of liquid nitrogen stood shoulder to shoulder in the corner and next to those was a sack barrow stacked with crates of lavender honey. Alderney watched as she stared up open mouthed at the array of stainless steel spatulas, spoons, tongs, whisks, ladles, sieves, mashers, muddlers, scrapers, graters and grinders hooked on a rail above their heads.

'Oooh, it's cold in here,' Keeley said, pulling her jacket tight.

'Why don't we have a little something to warm us up then? How about some hot chocolate?'

Keeley raised an eyebrow. 'I know you're old, but I didn't think you were inviting me back for a cup of cocoa.'

'Trust me,' said Alderney. 'You've never tasted hot chocolate like this before.'

And he was right. The spiced rum, fresh chilli and lime sugar mixed into the bitter chocolate drink masked the taste of the crushed Zopiclone tablets. He carried her to the marble slab at the far end of the workshop, like a father carrying his daughter to bed from the car late at night. Alderney wept silently as he got to work, licking the tears away with a tongue that did not seem to be his own.

The franchise deal for House of Finch was signed the following year. Soon there would be Houses of Finch in London, Tokyo, New York and Abu Dhabi, with more planned the following spring. Alderney put all thoughts of the girl to the back of his mind, concentrating instead on creating new and ever more adventurous flavours for his chocolates. But when he closed his eyes at night, he would see her sleeping innocently on the marble; his own personal Snow White. Except he had done what the huntsman never could. He wondered if her cat ever had those kittens.

Alderney drank. A lot. He took pills to help him sleep. Not Zopiclone, he told his doctor. Anything but that. He welcomed the dreamless sleep that came with the drugs, but inevitably they stopped working. And the day came, as he knew it would. Sweating chemicals from every pore, his face reddened with broken blood vessels, Alderney tossed and turned in his designer bedsheets, afraid to stay awake, frightened to fall asleep.

...the priest, the pyramid, the jungle and the sky were all gone. There was only black. The serpent spoke, his voice everywhere at once.

'I am hungry. Feed me.'

Alderney swung his feet over the side of the bed, the thick carpet cushioning his bloated frame. He trudged to the kitchen. The sleeping tablets he had washed down with a large measure of single malt gave him the sensation of being puppet master of his own body. The time lag between thought and movement was impossibly long. The arm reaching for the knife block seemed to cover a distance of many metres before his hand curled itself around the carbon-handled boning knife. As he thrust the blade up into the soft flesh below his sternum, Alderney caught his reflection in the window. His eyes were two dots of red. His tongue flicked out. The forked end quivered. Quetzalcoatl smiled.

He was going to feed.

BELLARMINE

Nathaniel Bird's hand shook with effort as he bent the final metal pin between finger and thumb, and dropped it onto the pile with the others. Twenty-five bent pins for the twenty-five cursed years his wife had walked God's earth. He unhitched his breeches and angled his manhood into the cooking pot on the floor. A stream of hot urine shot out onto the curved metal, splashing back over his shins. He gritted his teeth against the pain of a thousand thorns ripping through his cock. When the agonising flood had dried to a trickle, he gave himself a shake and stared at the flaccid monstrosity in his hand. Reeking and covered in sores, this was the latest way that bitch had decided to hex him. It was punishment for his visits to the local brothel, of course.

But what did she expect? If his wife wouldn't perform her sacred duties, what was a man to do?

If only he had seen the mark of Lucifer on her before they were wed. But she had been so beautiful, enchanting him with her evil ways, making him think she was sweet and virtuous. It was only when she had disrobed on their wedding night that he saw it. In the flickering candle glow, on the skin on inside of her thigh was a brown crescent moon shape; the bite of the Devil himself. The things his new wife had done with him, done to him, that night had made him think that maybe, just maybe, living with a succubus might not be too bad. She brewed her own beer too. So Nathaniel Bird put the birthmark far from his mind.

Until she failed to bear him a child. After a year with no sign of any offspring, Nathaniel decided she needed more of his seed, so he started to force himself upon her daily. The more she fought, the more excited he got. But still no baby came. After two years of fruitless endeavours, Nathaniel tried a different course of action. He would beat the evil out of his wife. But still, no baby came.

What kind of woman does not fall after three years of marriage? Only a truly wicked one, spoiled by her unholy union with Satan.

Thou shalt not suffer a witch to live.

But if he killed his wife, it would mean admitting to the whole village that he had been laying with a demon. He could not stand the shame. So he decided he would play that Devil's whore at her own game.

A length of shiny red ribbon and a scrap of rough leather lay on the table next to Nathaniel's gutting knife. He hacked the ribbon into four; one for each of her limbs. Next, he carved the shape of a heart into the leather. Finally, he dragged the edge of the knife along the pad of his thumb, slicing almost down to the white. A fat glob of blood oozed out, and he let it drip into the pot. With his other hand he threw in the leather heart and the ribbons. He had paid a pretty penny for that bright scarlet, and he hoped it would be worth it. When he was happy with the amount of blood mingling in with his foamy urine, he wrapped his thumb tightly with a rag before placing the pot on the fire.

He would teach that witch a lesson.

Let *her* be the one who burned when she pissed.

Let *her* flesh be pierced with pins the next time she refused him his marital right.

Let *her* heart be seized the next time she tried casting a spell on him.

Let all her wicked ways come back to her tenfold.

While he was waiting for the foul concoction to cook down, Nathaniel opened a bottle of his wife's famous beer and took a swig of the delicious nectar. Another reason not to kill the bitch. He quickly finished that bottle, and another, and another. All the while, the stinking brew bubbled away in the iron pot. Just one more bottle, thought Nathaniel Bird, then back to the task at hand.

Elizabeth's beer sold out early that day, so she pulled her cart back from the market slowly, dragging her feet with every step. If she had somewhere else to go, she would, but he would surely find her and force her to come home. As she walked, she thought back to her wedding day. How happy she had been, to be leaving the chaos of her family home. The eldest of twelve children, Elizabeth couldn't wait to be lady of her own manor, even if it was only a two room shack on the edge of the next village. Her mother and her many aunts had given her lots of advice in the months leading up to her marriage to Nathaniel Bird, the most notable being to make him happy.

'Keep your husband happy, you keep yourself blessed, my girl,' one of the oldest aunts had told her.

'But how do I keep a man happy?' Elizabeth remembered asking. She laughed ruefully to herself as she lugged the cart over a fallen tree-trunk. Of course she knew about the union between man and wife. She couldn't escape it sleeping in the same room as her mother and father, separated only by a thin curtain. An older cousin had taken Elizabeth to one side and told her of secrets dark and wet, of hidden places and ways to use her hands and mouth that made her face flush and her insides tingle.

As she rounded the final corner and saw smoke rising from the chimney of their house, Elizabeth's insides tingled again, this time with fear. He was home already. She braced herself for whatever indignities lay in store for her as she gingerly pushed the front door open.

Pungent black smoke filled the room. The smell reminded her of the tannery. Through the dense cloud, Elizabeth could see Nathaniel slumped in his chair, surrounded by empty bottles. On the table in front of her snoring husband, the hideous pottery face of a bellarmine jar leered at her. Nathaniel called her a witch and a whore of Satan and a demon, and a hundred other frightening things while he beat her, but now she knew he meant it. He really thought she was a witch.

Elizabeth had never seen a real bellarmine up close, so she tiptoed to the table to take a closer look. The bulging eyes of the clay face stared at her with spiteful hatred, the mouth open to reveal long, curved teeth. Known to some folk as witch-bottles, bellarmines were used to invert curses, sending pain, misfortune or even death to the witch responsible. Peering through the smoke coming from the cooking pot, Elizabeth could see her husband had left the bottle unfilled. Sitting in the tarry residue at the bottom of the pot were a stack of pins, a curled up rag and some thin pieces of brown string.

Moving closer, Elizabeth brushed one of the discarded beer bottles with her foot. Nathaniel's eyes flicked open, bloodshot and full of drunken rage. Without thinking, Elizabeth grabbed the clay jar by its long neck and swung it with all her strength into her husband's face. The bulbous end of the bellarmine smashed into Nathaniel's nose in a spray of shattered clay and blood. As his hand went up to his busted nose, Elizabeth's hand went for the gutting knife on the table and in one swift arc she sliced through the exposed part of his neck and across his wrist. Hot lifeblood splashed Elizabeth's face. She dropped the knife, staggered backwards and watched as her husband bled to slowly death. She may have never made her husband happy, but at last, she felt truly blessed.

The Disappearing

Mermaid

Slipping into the water causes goosebumps to erupt painfully on her skin. Despite the steam rising from the surface of the pool, the cold outside has penetrated deep into her bones. She loves being under the water, the safe calm and the quiet of it. On land, the harder she tries to disappear, the more visible she becomes. But in the water she is a nymph, a filigree seahorse unable to carry its young. As she swims, her arms are razor blades through silk. The apple she ate for breakfast sits heavily inside her. Despite having sliced it into quarters, then eighths, then sixteenths and peeled each slice slowly and deliberately with her dullest knife, the pieces of fruit have reassembled themselves into a polished jade sphere inside her. A waxy orb buffed to a synthetic shine, sagging like lead shot in her stomach. The drag increases with every stroke as she imagines the apple as a smooth, green anchor tied to her ankle with rusty barbed wire.

To put the enemy fruit to the back of her mind, she plays her favourite game, fantasising about the delicious delicacies that will form her last meal, the final feast before she disappears altogether. Not a feast as those greasy finger-lickers would understand it, gorging on stinking carcasses and sticky white bread, like eating filthy washing-up sponges. No, a noble feast. A terrifying and terrific feast. A feast she can only attempt when she reaches the pinnacle of weightlessness, floating through space untethered by flesh.

It will be laid out, waiting for her, spread like a lover under soft candle light.

First, an *amuse bouche* of a budding rose dipped in liquid nitrogen, forever caught before full bloom. Each tiny petal to be plucked with tweezers and placed on the tongue to slowly melt.

The starter; a single needle to be bent and swallowed. Repeat, until her tiny stomach is cold with metal. She imagines pulling a needle through the taut skin of her thighs, sewing them together. She is a mermaid, legs permanently fused, combing her thinning hair on a lone rock, far out at sea.

The *entrée* is always the trickiest course, but in her most recent daydreams she has settled on a porcelain platter as big as a dustbin lid, which grows as she approaches, as big as a table, now as big as the room, now so vast it curves with the horizon. The closer she gets, the more clearly she can see a black square in the middle of the white. Her hand reaches forward, her limb unfurling as long and graceful as an octopus tentacle. The world shrinks, and she is now standing in the centre of the dish with a tiny postage stamp of dark chocolate at her bare feet. As she lifts it to her mouth, the smell hits her nose and she imagines each miniscule particle of cocoa being absorbed into her bloodstream, bursting on impact with her red blood cells, releasing pure sweetness into her collapsing veins. The square in her hand is now the size of a paperback book, melting and oozing between her fingers. She drops it with a fat, heavy splat. Even her fantasies must show restraint.

Dessert, after the sickly promise of the main course, is clean and pure. A curved silver bowl, reflecting the slices of her cheekbones. The bowl is filled with shaved ice, frozen shards to be eaten from a spindly spoon with a handle of bone. She bites down on the ice, only to find it is broken glass and crushed diamonds. Crunching the granules like sugar causes her gums to bleed, dripping onto the sparkling snow to create a crimson raspberry slush that reminds her of a lonely and frightened child, who once sat on a pebble beach in a thunderstorm, ice cream melting in her hand. Her tears are invisible under the water, just as they mingled with those English summer raindrops.

And finally, a *digestif* to cleanse her palette and wash away her sins. A cut crystal goblet, a poisoned chalice with a sharpened rim. This is her favourite part of the imaginary menu, when her mind excels in masochistic delight. Sometimes the glass is filled with a warming brew of battery acid and turpentine. Other times, it is a shot of bleach, fizzing and frothing as she knocks it back in one. But today, the darling of all her fantasy cocktails, the goblet is filled to the brim with mercury. Thick and unctuous, cold and creamy, it coats her oesophagus as she drains the glass, dampening any last fire she has within.

Sinking to the bottom of the pool, the muffled echo of her jutting hipbone bumping onto the tiles wakes her from satisfied ecstasy. Too weak to muster any desire to resurface, she resigns herself to the knowledge that her final feast will be chlorine and silence.

Staring up through the blue, the mermaid smiles.

THE STORY OF

MOSES

Every kid in the Kennington Crew knew the story of Moses. Kicked out of school at ten, left to spend his days robbing tourists at knifepoint in Trafalgar Square. He earned his place in the gang by taking a vicious and prolonged beating that left him deaf in one ear. When he eventually got pulled by the Feds at age fourteen he had been 'going county' for two years, selling Class A to the bedsit dwellers of

Margate and Ramsgate. Moses spent more of his fifteenth year inside correctional facilities and young offender's institutes than out. And now, at just seventeen, he was a man before his time. For keeping his mouth shut and staying loyal to the gang on the inside, the Crew Elders made Moses boss of his own county line, with his own weight to shift and his own runners.

The northern coast of Kent was dotted with decaying seaside resorts; ghost towns inhabited by junkies and delinquent care home kids. Easy pickings for an enterprising young businessman like Moses. He avoided leaving the city if he could help it, but a small village on his patch had recently gone quiet. No requests for product, and no money coming back up the line. Three Youngers had been sent out to collect in two weeks and none had returned. Sometimes they got picked up by the Police, sometimes they went on a four-day crack binge and forgot what they were doing, and sometimes they just stopped playing drug-dealer and went back home to their mums.

The train journey to Dunwich-on-Sea was a mission. As council estates whizzed past the window, punctuated only by tiny pockets of park and woodland, Moses thought back to his first trip as a Younger. Every Younger wanted a chance to prove themselves to the crew, and this was the best way. Preparations for the journey began with a bottle of liquid laxative. On his way out to pick up the goods, his guts began to twang. This quickly escalated to a grumbling wobble pushing its way through his intestines, picking up speed until Moses had to squat under the concrete stairwell of his towerblock. He'd had barely enough time to pull his trackies down to his ankles before the whole world fell out of his ring.

When young Moses got to the flat, two capsules of diarrhoea medicine had been waiting for him. And finally, it was the Vaseline. One of the Elders in the crew had offered to help him as it was his first time, but he told them he was no batty-boy and lubed the clingfilm wrapped packages himself, shoving as many up there as he could stand. His sphincter was constantly contracting and cramping on the walk to the station. Moses remembered gritting his teeth when he passed the guards at the ticket barrier, certain one of them would notice the beads of perspiration leaping from his face. He had stared straight ahead, thinking of the box-fresh Nike Air Force Ones that were waiting for him, and not the twelve hundred quid's worth of heroin and crack secreted up his arse.

The train hissed into Dunwich station, the sound of the opening doors rousing Moses from his memories. The carriage filled with the seaweed tang of salty summer air. A faint aroma of rotten fish drifted in, but it was still better than the diesel fumes, rising damp and crack-smoke he was used to back in London. If he could get to the nest and find out what had happened to his money, Moses might even get to smoke a blunt on the beach before he had to get back. His crew exploited the disabled, the junkies and the whores, cuckooing their flats to sell their product, until the cops bust in and closed down the so-called nests. The tenants got evicted and slapped with an ASBO, and the dealers moved on to cuckoo some other sucker, too weak or too addicted to argue. Whores were the best. Those skets were always obliging with a toothless blowjob for a few rocks.

It wasn't until the train pulled away that Moses saw he was the only person on the platform. Having just an address on a scrap of paper, and no knowledge of the town itself, he walked down the ramp to the main road to jump in a cab. The taxi rank was deserted. A lone seagull whirled and cried in the sky. The calls of the gull echoed like laughter. Laughing at him. Mugging him off.

Muttering under his breath, Moses picked up a stone and launched it high up in the air, missing the seagull by a mile.

'I ain't getting owned by no beach pigeon.'

In answer, the bird squirted a glob of chalky-white shit on Moses' hoody.

The train station held an elevated position over Dunwich Bay. The sea below seemed flat despite the summer sun, a grey façade of ocean hiding what was beneath. He decided to head towards the beach in the hope that someone would call him on his pay-as-you-go burner phone. Blank-eyed houses stared him down as he walked. A curtain fluttered from one of the open windows. Moses jumped, then cussed himself for being a pussy.

Everyone knew he was a badman. They found out on the day of his arrest, those few short years ago. He had been pulled as he was about board the train back to the city. It took four Transport Police to ground him. Moses relished in the memory of smacking the fat station guard in the face before they took him down. He held out in custody for ten days before finally giving up the two grand in used notes tightly rolled and plugged up as high as his young fingers could reach.

Thinking back to that time, refusing all food and barely drinking any water, made his mouth dry. The rows of terraced cottages near the station had thinned to the odd wooden shed, and the pavement given way to a twisting path that led down to a shingle bay. A squat building with a flat roof stood alone at the top of the path. The angles of the building were off, and made Moses feel sick to look directly at it. Shiny buckets and spades swung on hooks around the door. A rack of postcards spun in the breeze. With any luck, he could buy a Coke and get directions to the nest. Ducking under a sun-bleached inflatable dolphin, Moses entered the shop.

The bright, friendly plastics were at odds with the antiquated goods stacked on the dusty shelves inside. Greying cardboard packets of *Hewson's Medicated Talc* stood next to cloudy bottles of aqueous cream and something called *Dr. William's Pink Pills*. The smell of rotten seaweed was stronger in here. There was no drinks fridge, or even any brand names that he recognised. About leave, Moses heard a cough from behind the counter. A round shape sat in the dark. He called out.

'You got any Coke?'

The figure behind the counter remained still.

'Oi, I'm talking to you. Do. You. Have. Any. Coke.'

Silence.

'Blud, I'm getting vex now. Get us a cold drink before I bus' up your shitty little shop.'

The figure stood with a snort. A sliver of sunlight illuminated the pale skin of a woman in a lumpy brown cardigan. She went into a back room, lifting a curtain and letting it slip behind her. The damp air in the shop was making Moses claustrophobic. But his tongue was like a dry sock in his mouth, and if the weirdo skank had gone to get him a drink, he could wait.

A few minutes later, the woman shuffled back through the curtain holding a swirled glass bottle. She placed the bottle on the counter without saying a word, and sat back down with a fat squelch.

Moses swiped the bottle and saw a hand written label that read 'Root Beer'. It was wet and cold, and he chugged the whole lot down in one. The taste reminded him of the pink cream his mum used to put on his cuts when he fell off his bike.

'You like?' came a croak from the shopkeeper.

'Yeah, I like,' Moses laughed, memories of his childhood softening his edges for a brief moment.

'Soda Stream.'

She smiled proudly, like she was introducing her favourite child.

'I'm looking for Adams Street. Do you know where it is?'

'Soda Stream,' she said again.

His eyes adjusting to the gloom, Moses could now see her wide, toad-like face, rubbery lips glistening with spit and bulbous eyes pointing in different directions. Having spent so long numb to the world, he was angry at this woman for making him feel something.

'Adams Street. Tell me where it is before I shank you, you mental bitch.'

'You're welcome,' came the reply.

'Fuck you, you crazy old derp.'

Moses half-heartedly kicked over a display of tinned pilchards. As he yanked open the door, the woman called after him.

'Shank you! Welcome! Shank you! Welcome!'

He slammed it behind him so hard he hoped the glass would break. It didn't.

Knowing he would have to risk using the burner phone, Moses pulled the chunky Nokia from his pocket.

No signal.

Whirling around in different directions, holding the phone in the air hoping to catch a few bars, he spun straight into a solid mass that knocked him to the ground. A massive column of a man, close to seven at the tip of his frayed top hat. Moses got to his feet, taking in the rubber boots, then the ragged, stripy trousers and the ill-fitting suit jacket.

'Mate, watch where you're going, yeah?' Moses' voice wavered.

The man remained silent, put his hand in his pocket and pulled out a long, pale fish. The fish gave a spasmodic twitch in his spade-like hand. At the same time, Moses pulled a short knife from his own pocket. A wet grin split the big man's face and he reached forward, plucking the shank from his hand as easily as picking a daisy. He raised the still jerking fish and jammed the knife into its grey belly. With a quick twist, the fish's guts flopped in a bloody mess of tubes and sacs onto Moses' trainers. Saliva flooded his mouth, but he was spared the final indignity of puking over himself by a solid blow to the back of his head.

Moses awoke, unable to move. He lifted his neck and a shriek of pain shot through his skull. His hands and feet were bound tight. It was dark, but the shingle shifting under his body as he tried to wriggle free told him he was on the beach. The whisper of the tide pulling over the pebbles was all he heard at first, but he soon detected an undercurrent of repetitive chanting. The voices ebbed and flowed with the sea in a language he didn't understand. Strings of vowels were broken by harsh, guttural growls and alien glottal stops.

'Nnnnnga'aaa.   Nnnnnga'aaa.   Eeeeeiaaa yog'oth. Eeeeeiaaa nnnnnnga'aaa.'

Gaining enough purchase to roll onto his side, he now had a full view of the procession of flames wending its way down the steep beach path. He strained to loosen his hands, the twine cutting into his skin, blood dripping from his wrists.

The train of shadows reached the beach, lead by the grinning circus freak with the fish. His top-hat was gone, replaced with a spindly crown. Behind him, each lit by their own flaming torch, were the inhabitants of Dunwich-on-Sea. Elongated heads, bulging eyes, skin glistening with ooze. They had reached the beach, and were staking the flaming torches in a semi-circle around Moses. As he pushed at the shingle with his feet, trying to inch himself away, one split from the group, crawling low to the ground in a skittering, lizard motion. It was a child, pale-faced yet green around the edges. She held out her hand to stroke his hair. Webbing stretched between her stubby fingers.

'Get fucked, you mingin' little sprong.'

He tried to kick out, but the child gave a swampy gargle and opening her mouth to display rows of tiny, razor sharp teeth before running into the arms of the now naked shop-keeper. Froggy warts covered her ancient shoulders, and two wrinkled breasts dangled limply from her chest. Her eyes glinted at Moses in the fire glow.

The head man stepped forward, fully naked. Flipper feet led to thick-set legs covered in silvery scales. Shiny scales also edged his well-defined torso. His phallus stood hard and proud in the dark. He approached slowly, knife in hand, eyes hungry. But instead of slitting Moses throat, he snipped the bonds that held his hands and feet, blood rushing into his extremities. The fizz of pins and needles prevented Moses from getting up and he stumbled around in front of the misshapen and slippery bodies of the amphibious abominations. Fish-faced frogboys and toad-women surrounded him. On every side were hunch-backed children and wizened old men with angry red gills on their necks. He tried to run but the circle tightened. Their chanting increased in intensity and volume as the group herded him towards the churning sea. The tide frothed like milk, thick with jellyfish and crabs. He wheeled round on the shingle as the chanting reached a crescendo, then dropped to a reverent hush. One of the naked throng behind him emitted an ululating cry. Their leader screamed, in a voice so unhuman it rendered Moses paralysed.

'The Great One no longer dreams! Rise from the deep, O Ancient One and receive your final sacrifice!'

The deafening roar of rusted metal came from the roiling sea, and an horrific mass emerged from the black, framed by the tips of its unfurling tentacles. Moses' trainers slid on the wet shingle as he scrambled back from the steaming, sulphurous water. He stretched an arm out to save himself, only to feel the needle-point snap of a mouth around his bloody wrist. Flicking his shoulder round, he flung the child into the path of the huge squid monster now looming before him. Her rag-doll body slammed into the face of the creature. It wiped out two of its devotees with a monstrous whip-crack of one massive tentacle. Another suckered limb curled around the broken body of the child, tossed it up in the air and caught her in its ferocious beak with a brittle crunch. The shop-keeper wailed as bloody shards of child bone littered the beach.

Moses ran, spraying shell and pebble in his wake as he dodged the fish-people now swaying on their knees in front of their octopus deity. He ignored the burning in his limbs as he ran the depth of the beach, but was unable to ignore the cries of agony, the sound of breaking bones and cracking cartilage that followed. He didn't look back until he reached the top of the cliff. When he finally turned to survey the scene on the beach below, the tide was lapping gently over the mangled naked bodies strewn at the water's edge. The sea was calm, with no evidence of the boiling, poisonous soup it had been minutes before.

When Moses found his way back to the station the train was waiting, doors open, lights on, devoid of passengers. He jumped on at the first carriage and walked the length of the train sealing himself in by pressing the door close buttons before the train finally trundled its way back to London.

Every kid in the Kennington Crew knew the story of Moses.

He swore off ever going county again, mumbling something about inbreds and poisoned Germolene. His dreams were plagued with seas like treacle, thronged with deformed frogs leaping from the waves onto a beach made of crushed bones. He tried to stay awake with uppers, only to find the dreams seeping into his reality. Sticky tentacles reached for him from every cupboard door. He recoiled from smiling children. Walking down a dark stairwell, he would find himself ankle-deep in water teeming with frenzied silver-grey fish, tying themselves in knots and eating their own tails. At age eighteen he boarded his final train to Beachy Head, where he took a free-fall from the cliffs.

The Youngers say he called out to the sea on his way down, but none can agree on what he said.

The Elders all said it was a waste. He made good money.

The Old Ones welcomed Moses home, under the deep, to dream for eternity in the cold, black waters of his tomb.

FOR THOSE IN PERIL

ON THE SEA

We were so confident in sealing the deal, the journey to Paris was First Class on the Eurostar with champagne and caviar all the way. By the time we arrived in France, Renners was so plastered he could barely stand up. But it didn't matter, it was a foregone conclusion, all we had to do was get the papers signed and we had closed the biggest land sale in Kent history.

'Johnno,' he slurred as we wobbled out of the Gare du Nord 'We're gonna be rich. Filthy, stinking rich. Not bad for a couple of twats from Strood.'

Seven hours later, I was staring at my reflection in the black glass of a ferry window. I could feel the tension radiating from Renners. The lurch of the waves pulled at my guts. The champagne from this morning sloshed around inside, hollow and bitter. I'd told him I could take the papers, that I could handle meeting low level European royalty on my own, but he insisted on coming. Said it would look better for the firm if they didn't send a junior. I didn't want to point out that I was about to be made a partner. He had twenty years on me and had a way of looking at you, like he could turn in a second.

'I need some air'

I stood and staggered as the floor pitched. The dimly lit bar might have been sophisticated once. Now faded faux-velvet armchairs with foam poking through at the seams clustered sadly around sticky tables. Bottles clinked gently as a solitary barman stocked the fridge. Who the bottles were for, I couldn't say. I hadn't seen another soul since we boarded. This was a lorry driver's ferry, we had seen them queued up nose to tail at the port. They must keep to themselves, somewhere dank and sweaty below.

We had been due to meet our client in The Hotel de Crillon at 3pm.

3pm came and went

4pm came and went.

At half past four, I went outside for a smoke. I didn't have to, this was Paris where everyone puffed away wherever they liked, but I needed some space from Renners and his constant foot-tapping and pen-clicking. He must have realised it was annoying me, because all his nervous tics had disappeared by the time I got back from chain smoking three Gauloises. Another hour passed before a slick-haired waiter appeared carrying a silver platter, bearing a single white envelope.

'From Monsieur DeVille.'

He placed the platter on the table. I leaned over to pick up the envelope, but Renners snatched it from my hands.

'My friends,' he began reading in his irritating, nasal voice. 'It is with greatest apologies that I am unable to continue with this purchase as we agreed. Due to unforeseen circumstances, I must be in London. I will meet with you tomorrow at The

Albemarle Hotel in Piccadilly, where we can further discuss our business. I have made arrangements for your return journey.'

I traversed the carpeted corridor of the boat, listing to the side to keep balance. I still had yet to see another passenger. Probably all in the toilets throwing up. I knew how they felt. I pushed open a reinforced glass door against the wind and found myself out on deck, sea spray blasting my face. There was no moon, but I could just make out the churning water below lit by the emergency lights. Sliding about on the slick deck, being pushed along by the wind, I decided to go back inside. Sitting in silence with Renners for three hours was preferable to being out in a squall wearing only mid-priced pinstripe. Gripping onto the plastic bucket seats I managed to make my way back to the door and was about to go inside when something swooped over my head. I looked up in time to see a black shape disappearing onto the deck above. I was sure I had seen the shape of wings, but no sea bird would be out in this weather.

At night.

My heart thudded on the inside of my now sodden shirt. Slamming the door behind me, back in the cossetting warmth of the corridor I quickly came to my senses. It was gale force out there. The swoop I felt must have been some bit of cross channel junk blowing about in the wind. As I walked to the bar, I had almost convinced myself that I had seen some ties loose on the railings, that a life-belt had come free and a sudden gust had blown it up above my head. And that the sound I heard over the roar of the sea was not the flap of leathery wings.

I needed a drink.

Back in the bar, I found the drinks menu printed on an A4 sheet of paper that promised 'The Finest Slovakian Wines'. I never normally drink wine, but this appeared to be all they stocked. I looked about for the barman, but even he appeared to have deserted us.

'He said to help ourselves and leave the money on the bar,' croaked Renners, slumped in a booth with an empty wine glass in front of him and half-drunk bottle of red on the table. I grabbed one of the glasses hanging above the bar.

Renners was staring mournfully at DeVille's note.

'The deal isn't blown, don't worry,' I said, hoping to lift his spirits. 'We'll get him tomorrow.'

I plucked the note from his fingers. I had expected to see gothic handwriting, perhaps a wax seal. The signature at the bottom was executed with a flourish, but other than that it was a standard laser-print letter.

'I wonder how he knew we didn't have a return ticket for the Eurostar?'

We had wrongly assumed we would be celebrating in style, our commission from the sale being enough to fly back on a private jet if we so desired. My colleague poured me a glass and stayed silent. He left his empty. Good job too, he didn't look well.

'I think he's playing mind games with us, trying to get us to drop the price.'

'It's not about the money.' Renners' voice was tight.

'Of course it is. Everything is about the money.'

'Not for him...' Renners slapped a hand over his mouth.

I jumped back in my chair, out of the firing line in case he chucked up. He was pale. Sweat beads dangled off his eyebrows. The hand clamped firmly over his mouth looked waxy, his nails dark.

'Are you alright? You look sick.'

'I'm just hungry.'

'I'll see if I can find that barman, order us some food.'

I was glad to get out of the bar. He must have been seasick and hungover as Hell, but Renners was giving me the creeps. Back out on the empty hallways again, the constant vibration of the engines had my teeth on edge. Even if I could find someone to make us some food, I wasn't sure I would be able to keep it down. At the far end of the corridor was a door marked 'Lorry Bays'. The drivers must have somewhere to get a fry-up. I opened the door and stepped onto a metal staircase, the bare walls and functional lights in stark contrast with the shabby glamour of the ferry interior. I began clanking down the steps until I got to the next level, opened the door to Lorry Bay 1 and poked my head through. To my surprise there were no cabs, just a row of metal containers. That might explain why the ferry was so deserted. The drivers must have deposited their cargo and driven away.

We couldn't be the only passengers.

I ran down the metal stairs to Lorry Bay 2, and opened a door to the same scene. No trucks, just containers. The ferry lurched to its side and I had to grab hold of the balustrade to stop myself falling to the floor below. I heard a loud clang, and looked down to see one of the container doors swinging in rhythm with the motion of the waves.

'Hello?'

No reply.

I jumped down the steps two at a time and peered into the open container. A draught of cold air blew out, and I managed to catch the door before it swung back and hit me. The inside stank of mouldy basements and potato dirt. A solitary tea chest was pushed to the very back. I could just about make out the 'this way up' sign through the gloom. I had come this far, and even though my stomach was starting to growl, I needed to know what was in the box. I jumped up into the container, a foetid smell filling my nostrils. As soon as I had both feet inside, the door slammed behind me with a deadly thud.

Plunged into absolute darkness, I blinked hard and put my hands out in front of me, turning slowly to face the door. I took what I thought was the two steps necessary to make contact with the cold metal, but all I felt was air. I tried to keep still and re-set my internal compass. I was certain I could hear breathing. Surely my own, echoing off the interior of the container.

I held my breath.

Silence.

My own heartbeat in my ears.

I let my breath out. At the same time a sudden ragged gasp came from behind me. I launched myself forward, falling through the door and back into the blinding light of the lorry bay. Scrabbling to my feet, I didn't look behind me as I clattered up the steps and slammed the deck door. I ran all the way back to the bar, carpet thudding dully beneath my shoes.

I burst through the swing doors, expecting to see Renners slumped over the table where I left him, but the bar appeared abandoned. A glass swayed in its hook over the bar, catching my eye.

'Renners? There was someone, in one of the containers. In the lorry bay...'

As I was saying it, I could already picture a poor Eastern European lorry driver, deprived of sleep since he left his depot, crawling into one of his cargo containers to catch a nap before he had to resume his journey across the continent. I leaned over the bar, feeling like an idiot. Renners was on his hands and knees next to the drinks fridge.

'Have they got beers?' I said. 'I don't think I can handle any more red.'

The back of his head was twitching. I saw two pairs of legs, one kneeling with feet clad in leather loafers and another pair, stretched out underneath Renners, attached to a lifeless body. I yelped as he spun his head at an unnatural angle, piercing me with bloodshot eyes. Strings of flesh hung from his canines, now transformed into elongated sabres. Blood dribbled from his lips. Arterial spray from the dead barman beneath him covered his chalky face and splattered his shirt.

'The Master is coming!' he howled. 'And He has promised to make me immortal.'

Renners screeched after me as I staggered backwards. 'Take what he offers you, Johnny. He will only offer it once…'

I could no longer see his head over the top of the bar, but I heard his greedy crunching and slurping as I tumbled backwards through the doors.

'He speaks the truth,' drifted a voice from the corridor.

There was no-one there.

The lights flickered.

'Help, wait, help!' I babbled as I raced after the voice. Rounding the corner, the voice came again.

'A once in a lifetime offer.'

It was coming from upstairs. I ran until I found myself in a small arcade, packed wall to wall with fruit machines. The only light came from the flashing cherries and golden barrels of the one arm bandits.

'Who are you? My friend…he…'

'Ahh, yes. He is my friend now, I think.' He sounded close. I could detect a slight accent. The 'r' rolled cruelly over his tongue.

'I'm calling the Police,' I yelled weakly.

'We are on the sea, yes? Who will come? You are alone in your peril. The only one who can save you is me.'

I followed the voice to the farthest corner of the room. A Castlevania game stood alone in the dark, the screen blank.

'Who are you?'

'Oh, I have many names. Some know me as Orlock. Some as Vlad Tepes. You know me as DeVille. That is not important. What is important is what I am going to offer you now.'

The shadow beside the video game unfolded itself into the shape of a man. His broad shoulders tapered down to a slim waist and long legs. His face was still in darkness.

'Hear me,' DeVille whispered inside my head.

'See me.'

He stepped into the blinking light. His skin was white, all the paler in contrast with his neat, black triangular beard. His eyes, ringed with violet smudges, had the same bloodshot tinge that I had seen in Renners. His long hair was slicked back on his head, displaying long, thin ears. Everything about him seemed stretched and unnatural.

'I can give life to your dreams. Deliver your very heart's desire.'

I was unable to tear my eyes from his mouth. It moved at a different speed to the words coming from it, like he was caught in a satellite delay. His teeth glinted. His lips glistened. His voice was smooth and sibilant. My eyelids were heavy. My feet melted into the floor like hot glue.

Everything went black.

When I opened my eyes, I was facing a bank of dials, buttons and levers on a vast console. Lifting my head I could see rain battering a wrap-around window. I was high up over the deck, and judging by the instruments I guessed I was on the bridge. I tried to stand, but my wrists and ankles were lashed to a chair. I twisted in my seat, causing the whole chair to spin.

I was not alone.

Another man was tied to a large leather seat next to me. His white shirt and braided epaulettes indicated he was the Captain. He saw me and his eyes widened behind metal rimmed glasses. He was gagged but began to grunt and scream, thrashing his head about against the chair.

'Calm down,' I hissed, but this just made him chuck himself around even more. His eyes were focussed on the space above my head.

'It's him, isn't it? He's here.'

I spun the chair, but instead of the aquiline nose and clipped beard of DeVille, there was a woman.

'Oh, thank Christ,' I panted, trying to pull my arms free. 'Some nutter has tied us up in here. Can you help?'

The woman said nothing. With a sinking heart I took in her waxy complexion, raven hair and black cherry lips. She smiled with a predatory glint in her bloodshot eyes, as two more women stepped out from behind her, flanking her on each side. Three impossibly beautiful yet strangely repulsive creatures stood before me. I could hear the Captain's terrified shrieks plunge to a resigned moan. The woman on the left of the trio had pale straw hair to match her milky skin. She fixed her watery blue eyes behind me, and before I could register, she was gone. There was the sound of ripping linen, then gargling and sucking. I tried to wrench myself out of the chair, and in an instant the right-hand woman was on me, her face inches from mine, long red hair cascading over my shoulders. Her breath stank of rancid meat. And yet, as she began to grind her hips against mine, something stirred.

'Yessss…' she whispered. 'Yessss. It's easy. So easy. That's right.'

Her tongue tickled my ear, blocking out the wheezing death throes of the Captain. I closed my eyes. Both her hands were in my hair. I felt my zip slowly being pulled down. I jerked my eyes open and saw the black-haired woman was now knelt between my thighs.

'Thissss can all be yours. We can be yours forever.'

A cold hand snaked into my boxer shorts. I felt the delicate touch of a tongue, then the threatening yet exhilarating brush of teeth on skin.

'No!' I yelled and slammed by head forward, smashing the red-head in the nose. She yelped and leapt three feet in the air. Her hands were now claws, buried deep into the felt covered ceiling. She clung on lizard-like, defying gravity. A drip of blood fell from her busted nose onto my face, giving me a buzz of triumph.

It was short lived.

My head jolted back as the snowy woman grabbed my hair and yanked. My neck was exposed to the hungry mouth of the gothic beauty between my knees and she lunged upwards. I screwed my eyes tight and braced for the slash to my throat which never came. The weight suddenly lifted from my legs, I heard a howl and a thud. I opened my eyes to see the broken body of the woman crumpled against the wall of the control room. Still conscious, despite the odd angle of her neck, she glared malevolently at me from the floor.

'Please accept my apologies. My pets are not quite house trained. A shame. They are such beauties, do you not think?'

DeVille was perched nonchalantly on the console, picking at his teeth with an exquisitely curved pinky nail. Wind and rain buffeted the glass behind him.

'What are you people?' I croaked. Blondie still had hold of the back of my head, my vocal chords like overtuned violin strings about to snap.

'We are what you could be. We are your potential. I can make you more than you are. I can give you life eternal.'

A clicking noise drew my attention away from DeVille's grand speech and back to the woman in the corner. One of her feet was on back to front and her arm was hanging down limply at her side. Unable to put weight on either, she kept slipping as she tried to stand. Her pre-Raphaelite friend scuttled down from the ceiling and took her good arm, leading her off the bridge. That left me, DeVille, the snowflake with her hands around my neck and the bloody mess that now passed for the Captain.

'If that's what immortality looks like, I think I'll pass. Thanks all the same.'

'As you wish,' DeVille nodded sagely. 'I can see you are a harder negotiator than your old friend. That is good. Money, women, eternal life, everlasting power. Name your price.'

'Price for what? The Abbey?' He was right, I was a better negotiator than Renners, and if I had to bargain my way off this ferry with my life, then so be it.

'Carfax Abbey? Yes, that is part of the deal. That, and your soul.'

A huge wave slammed against the window.

'My soul? What could you offer that would be enough to give you my soul?'

'You tell me. What is a good price for something you can't feel, can't see, hear, touch or taste?' He licked his thin lips.

'Why do you need my soul anyway? Why don't you just kill me?'

'Why do *you* need your soul? Answer me this, Jonathan.'

The storm outside was whipping the sea into angry pyramids of water crashing onto the deck. The floor was now violently rising and falling as the ferry corkscrewed over the waves. DeVille was still leaning against the control desk, as if we were drifting across a serene millpond.

I decided to make an opening offer.

'If you need the Abbey, I can make sure you get it for whatever price you like, to compensate you for not getting my soul.'

'I will have the Abbey for whatever price *you* like, to compensate *you* for the loss of your soul.'

'Whatever price I like? Anything at all?'

DeVille stood, spreading his arms wide. The grip on my throat loosened, and the pale woman appeared at his side, nuzzling around his thighs like a cat.

'Anything at all,' he whispered.

'And if I say no?'

He sighed, leaned lazily across the console and flicked a switch. Red lights began blinking all over the desk. A radio crackled. DeVille placed a finger on the receiver and the radio went dead.

DeVille shook his head.

'You had the world in your palm, Jonathan. I could have made you a God. Now you will beg me for your life. How sad for you. How disappointing for me.'

'Without me, you won't get The Abbey.'

Darkness rippled over his eyes, momentarily breaking the calm façade. He had shown his hand. The deal was mine.

'So, let's talk about price again shall we…'

The Ramsgate Herald, 18th July 2016

Demeter Ferries Disaster

The Demeter Ferry company has ceased trading with immediate effect following the ferry collision disaster at the weekend. Little is known about the full circumstances of the incident, in which the vessel steamed into the harbour wall at high speed. The captain is believed to have deserted his post. Meteorologists reported unseasonably bad weather in the channel for the time of year, with a localised squall hitting land the same time as the ferry crash. Sources state that there was only one survivor; a Mr. R. M. Renfield, who was conveyed to a nearby hospital, and unavailable for comment at time of print. The passenger manifest left one soul unaccounted for; a Mr Jonathan Harker.

Land Sale Announcement, 20th July 2016

Land registry records the sale of Carfax Abbey and attached lands to Count DeVille, of Romania, for an undisclosed sum.

THE MERMAID'S PURSE

'I've had enough of this shit.'

The rock-pooling trip was not going well. She had spent the last half-hour rolling her eyes and tapping away on her phone. Mikey had found nothing more than a single, pitiful crab.

'I'm bored,' she said. 'I'm going to the pub.'

Mikey watched as his mother stomped back to the beach, shouting over her shoulder.

'Why can't you just play in the penny arcade like a normal kid?'

She was right. He wasn't like the other kids. He picked his way after her, jumping between the shallow pools. The crab in the bottom of his bucket bobbed about as seawater slopped over his trainers. They were at least one size too small and molten blisters made him wince with every step. With a mind to give up and head to the pub garden, where he hoped a packet of crisps and a can of warm pop would be waiting, Mikey spotted a black jewel glinting in the sunlight. It was oblong and about the size of his hand, with a shiny bubble in the centre. A curved tendril sprouted from each corner giving it an alien, beetle-like quality. He knew what it was. Better than any crab. Better than pirate treasure even.

It was a mermaid's purse.

Holding it up to the light, Mikey could just make out the shape of a baby shark, smaller than his little finger and flicking its minuscule tail against the confines of the egg case. He dumped the crab without a second thought and carefully placed the mermaid's purse in the bucket with a covering of fresh seawater and a few fronds of seaweed.

That night, lying under a scratchy sheet trying not to hear his mum's headboard banging on the wall next door, Mikey couldn't stop thinking about the baby shark. He had hidden it under his fold-out bed when they got back from the pub. Mum hadn't noticed. She was too busy with the sweaty slob who had been plying her with cider all night. He pulled the plastic bucket out and stared at the floating black sac. He imagined the shark growing inside. He imagined it tearing through the leathery skin of the purse with its teeth, ripping a hole in the side of the bucket and sending a torrent of sea-water cascading through the corridors of the B&B. Naked holiday-makers running screaming from their rooms, struggling to breathe as the flood pulled them under. His mother and the greasy pig on top of her washed away, spinning and tumbling, bones smashing as the tide dragged them down the stairs, through the door, along the beach and out to the ocean, never to be seen again.

Mikey had quite an imagination.

The next morning, Mum was still asleep when he got up, quietly packed his rucksack and tiptoed downstairs for some breakfast. When he asked the landlady if he could make himself a bacon sandwich to take away, she looked down at him with a frown.

'It's for my mum. She's not feeling too well and...'

'Where did you get that bruise, love?'

Mikey's hand instinctively went up to his left cheek, where a yellow ghost lingered from the week before.

'Fell over,' he mumbled.

The landlady pursed her lips and hurried off to the kitchen, returning with the bacon sandwich plus a packed lunch in a Tupperware box.

'There you go, love. Safe journey.'

It will be now, thought Mikey. He shoved the sandwiches into his rucksack, scoffed the slice of sponge cake and launched the apple into the bushes. Then he tenderly poured the mermaid's purse and seawater into the lunchbox, closed the lid and waited for his mother to surface so they could catch the train home.

Mikey rushed to his bedroom when they got back to the flat, slammed the door and ripped the lid off the Tupperware releasing a thick, fishy odour. He breathed in deeply. The smell of the sea, so out of place twelve floors up, made his tummy flip over. The shark had grown on the journey, he was sure of it. Tiny fins strained against the edges of the bubble. No fluid could be seen inside the egg case now. It was all shark.

Mum went out as soon as she had unpacked and re-applied her make-up, leaving Mikey to scavenge whatever he could find for dinner. He was just sitting down to a cold tin of out of date ravioli when he heard a splash from his bedroom. Bounding through the door, he found his little friend thrashing and snapping its way out of the tattered egg case. The flapping of the distressed baby shark had displaced most of the water from the lunchbox. Mikey panicked, only now worrying how he was going to keep the fish alive so far from the sea. He ran to the kitchen and found a huge saucepan, filled it with tap water and dumped in all the salt from the shaker on the table. Mikey carried the pan back to his room, his matchstick arms wobbling with the strain. Gently transferring the shark to the pan with both hands, he could sense the coiled potential within its smooth flanks.

'Don't worry,' Mikey whispered as he placed the shark gently in the saucepan. 'I'll look after you.'

The shark circled his new territory, prowling the edges of the pan with a flicking tail. Mikey sat up and watched him swimming round until midnight, when he heard his mum's key in the front door. He jumped into bed and pretended to be asleep. She didn't check in on him.

Every morning, while Mum was sleeping off her hangover, Mikey rushed to his wardrobe where he had hidden the shark. He was feeding him on dried goldfish flakes from under the sink. The goldfish had been a gift from Dad, back when he still used to visit once in a while. He had proudly named him Frank. Mum had come home with a man one night, and Mikey heard her laughing and shouting, 'No! You can't do that' but giggling all the while. In the morning, six-year old Mikey found Frank floating belly-up in a tank filled with stale lager and cigarette butts.

He sprinkled a handful of flakes into the water. The shark, now a sleek grey bullet with black tips on each fin, ignored the food. He had bright, beady eyes, not dead black ones like the shark in Jaws, and he stared from the pan with a malevolent glare. Mikey didn't need to speak shark to understand the message.

No more flakes, Mikey.

Tentatively opening a dusty can of tuna he had found at the back of the cupboard, Mikey dropped few crumbs into the pan. The shark greedily hoovered it up, champing his ragged razor-wire teeth up and down. After that, he fed the shark a spoonful in the morning and a spoonful at night. Instead of smelling like crusty tissues and stale armpits, his bedroom now reeked of fish, both dead and alive. He was soon shoplifting two cans of tuna a day from the corner shop, as well as his usual chocolate bars and penny chews.

The shark was almost a foot long. He had outgrown the pan and needed a new home. The only thing Mikey could think of was his old paddling pool. He remembered splashing about on the balcony, naked and happy, with his parents smiling and laughing together. The paddling pool had been crumpled into a ball and shoved in the outside cupboard when Dad left. He opened the door and reached into the dark. Spiders dropped down onto his bare arm and unknown creatures tickled his fingers. Fighting every urge to recoil, he rooted around blindly until he made contact with the cold rubber of the pool. It was covered in mildew. He dragged it through the house leaving streaks of grime on the bare boarded floor. Mikey was seeing stars after blowing the thing up, with a mouth full of dust. The shark could sense change was afoot and he swam in eager circles, his teeth bared in a snaggle-toothed grin. Plucking him gently out of the cooking pot, Mikey held the shark up level with his face. The shark stared back.

'This is your new home, but please don't bite it or you might die.'

Silent and inscrutable though the shark was, Mikey was sure he gave a solemn nod as he released him into the paddling pool. He remembered hearing something about fish growing to the size of their surroundings and hoped it was true. The shark became sleeker and more sinister with every inch he grew.

One morning, up before dawn to feed the shark his breakfast, Mikey cut his finger on the tuna can. A single drop of blood fell into the water. The shark flicked around and pointed his long snout at the blood, now slowly sinking in the water like a wisp of red smoke. He orbited the dot, making Mikey feel dizzy. Another spot dripped from his finger, and the shark went into snapping, thrashing frenzy. Dirty water soaked into the carpet. The next day when he threw half a tin of tuna into the pool, the shark swam underneath it and tossed it up in the air with a splash before swimming away in disgust.

There were only three more days of summer left, and Mikey didn't have any of the necessary equipment that he needed for his first day of secondary school. No uniform. No pencil case. No shiny black shoes. No scientific calculator. At midday, he knocked lightly on her bedroom door.

'Mum…Mum.'

No answer.

'Mum. I need some money to buy things for school.'

'Fuck off. I'm asleep.'

'But Mum, I need…'

'I told you, I'm asleep. Leave a list on the table and I'll see what I can do. Now, piss off.'

Knowing that was the best he was going to get, Mikey stuck his head round his bedroom door.

'I'll get you some real food, don't worry' he cooed to the shark.

I know you will, Mikey, came the reply in his head. *You're a good boy.*

Sneaking through the back alleys of the nearby new-build estate, Mikey popped his head over garden fences and through hedges, trying to decide whether a shark would rather eat rabbit or guinea pig. He came to a garden with a high gate. Pushing his eye up to a knot in the wood he saw lily pad flowers in bloom, bright white and bubble-gum pink against the black water of a pond too beautiful to look at. Mikey was a scrawny kid and he easily squeezed himself through the thin opening between gate and fence. Staying close to the shadows, he crept closer to the house. Satisfied that all windows and doors were shut, and not seeing or hearing anyone, Mikey pulled the plastic bags from his pocket and got to work.

It was past dinner time when he got home. There was a note on the kitchen table.

Here's your school stuff. Gone for a curry,

Mum

In a pile on the chair were a two greying shirts, a single threadbare jumper and a pair of grey trousers with a hole in the knee. On closer inspection, all had labels sewn in them bearing different names. A couple of biros stolen from the bookies instead of the fountain pen he asked for. And the final insult; not a brand new rucksack, but a battered old briefcase. He had finished primary school as the weird kid who smelled of piss and never had new trainers. Now he was starting secondary school as the weird kid who smelled of fish and carried a briefcase. Throwing the clothes across the room and kicking the briefcase so hard he hurt his foot, Mikey scooped up the two plastic bags he had left by the front door and made his way to the bathroom.

The thunder of the taps filling the bath filled Mikey's ears, drowning out the lightning inside his head. How could she do this to him? Why did she hate him so much? Mikey already knew the answer. The older he got, the more he reminded her of Dad, and for this he had to be punished. Once the bath was full, Mikey upended the first plastic bag. A black and orange koi carp plopped into the water, followed by a second, dazzling and silvery-white, both stunned and still.

Entering his room, Mikey was intoxicated with the stench of rotting fish. He reverently picked the shark up, stroking its sleek flanks. He put his face to the dorsal fin, rubbing his cheek along its edge.

'Time for dinner,' he whispered.

The shark demolished the koi in a rabid frenzy of ripping scales and flesh. The skeletons of the fish revealed, blood and fish guts filled the tub. When the orgy of feeding was done, the shark was happy and full. Mikey was hungry and tired. Tired of it all.

He heard his mum stumble through the door in the early hours, tripping over her feet as she made for the toilet.

When the sound of her screams had died down, Mikey crept into bathroom. Through the gloom he could see blood splattered up the tiles and soaking the shower curtain. He climbed into the tub, letting the delicious warmth surround him. He put his arms around the shark and slept.

The first responders found the boy clinging to his mother's brutally ripped and ragged corpse in a bath full of coagulating blood. The attending detectives hypothesised a crazed partner, or even pimp, had committed the horrific crime. No murder weapon was ever found and the post mortem was inconclusive. The final reports painted a tragic picture of abuse, with all the usual hallmarks of neglect — no food in the cupboards, filth on the floors and walls, evidence of heavy drinking and drug use. All depressingly common, and despite the initial horror of the bloody murder scene, the case was soon forgotten.

Forgotten by everyone apart from a young Crime Scene Investigator, straight out of college, who knew how it felt to be a hungry child. Tasked with sweeping the house from top to bottom for any evidence of a murder weapon, she found a desiccated but intact shark egg case, hidden under the boy's bed. When the CSI held it up to the light she saw the tiny, unmistakeable shadow of a dead baby shark inside.

Poor little guy, she thought, *he never stood a chance.*

Brick Lane

BOOK SHOP

is an independent bookshop on
Brick Lane, London. Est. 1978

Fiction

London Books

Non-Fiction

New Titles

Children's Books

Poetry

Travel

Classics

Philosophy

Cards & Gifts

& more...

www.bricklanebookshop.org

Brick Lane Bookshop
(Eastside Books Ltd)
166 Brick Lane
London
E1 6RU

0207 247 0216
@bricklanebooks
www.bricklanebookshop.org

HERE BE MONSTERS

I'm going to tell you a story of the old times, child. Come in here, close by the flames. I will tell you of when the moon shone her ivory gaze down upon us, back when the sky was not sick.

The moon was a lady, Gramma?

They used to talk of the man in the moon, my little one. But no man could have glowed so gentle and kind. The sun must surely be a man, for he burns all he touches.

Tell me about the old times, Gramma. Tell me about when the monsters came.

Oh, you want to know about monsters, do you? I think you might be too young.

I'm not, Gramma. I've seen ten snows.

Child, what do you know of snow? In the old times, the snow was white. White as the moon, white as the clouds.

Don't be silly, Gramma, everyone knows clouds are grey like rivers, or yellow like teeth, or purple like blood or black like the sea. But never white.

Have you ever heard of rainbows, child?

Rain? Like the kind that burns?

No, rainbows, little one. See here, in this puddle. The oil shining on the surface, making colours.

Shimmers, Gramma?

Shimmers. Well, we used to have shimmers in the sky, called rainbows. Before the monsters.

Why did they come, Gramma?

Who?

The monsters.

It all started when I was not much older than you are now. I was playing in the garden...

What's a gar-den, Gramma?

A place where things grow.

Nothing grows now, does it Gramma?

Only you child, only you.

What happened to you in the gar-den?

I heard a sound. A sound I had never heard before. I looked up into the sky, shielding my eyes from the brightness.

What did you hear, Gramma? Was it monsters?

It was a humming, whirring, purring sound. It got louder and louder until my head hurt, and I lay on the grass and closed my eyes tight.

Were you scared, Gramma?

No, child. There was a voice. It told me not to be afraid. It was a voice like mothers, like hot chocolate and blankets. And I was not afraid.

But the monsters, Gramma. Did you see them, did you see them?

Oh I saw them in the end, child. Hundreds, thousands of swarming monsters.

What did they look like?

Now, you're getting ahead of yourself. I didn't see anything at first. No-one did. We just heard the voices telling us not to be afraid, that they were coming soon and not to hide.

But Gramma, what did you do? You have to hide from the monsters, everyone knows that. Even little five snows like Annie know that.

Ssh, don't wake her, she's had a long day. We all have.

But I'm right aren't I Gramma? We must hide from the monsters. That's what Mommy always told us. Before she went away.

Yes, and Mommy was right, child. We must hide from the monsters. But we didn't know that back then.

What was it like, when they came?

There was a lot of smoke, and fire in the sky. Your eyes burned and you itched all over and your throat was full of blood and grit.

What did the monsters want, Gramma?

To hurt. To kill. Nothing more, nothing less. Same as now.

What was that, Gramma? I heard a noise, out there. Monsters!

Hush now, it's just the wind.

But Gramma, look at the fire. There's no wind. It is monsters, I know it.

Then I had better finish my story quickly. You asked about the monsters? I will tell you about the monsters. After The Final War, when the few of us that were left came out of our bunkers and caves, we started to see them. Their bodies, broken and impaled on trees. Lying in the road, mangled and burned. They were covered in what we guessed was blood, but other things too. Things that were growing from inside them, bursting out like spring blooms reaching for the light. Their faces, those that were not destroyed, were so much like our own and yet so different. Peaceful somehow, in death. Their eyes, open for eternity, were blue. Blue like that sky on the day when I played in my garden.

The monsters...

No, child. They were no more monsters than you or Annie. No, the monsters were already here, on Earth. They...wait. Ssh. Quick, stamp out the fire. Don't make a sound.

Gramma...what is it?

Monsters.

Under

The Fringe Tree

Meet me under the fringe-tree

When the sun dips behind the barn

And the evening air darkens

Cold caressing your skin

I will be there

Where grancy grey-beard blossoms brush the ground

As the first blush of summer blooms on your cheek

I will be there

Let us spread on the hard earth

The sunken warmth of the day soothing our aches

Scorched grass tickling our ears

Let us show our scars to the stars

Let us not be afraid of what is to come

Meet me at the high tide

We can dance until dawn on the sand

And plan our escape

Waves rush over rocks

Smoothing their edges

Salt cleaning wounds

Hide in caves and in rock pools

Where no-one can hurt us

Let us steal a rowboat and sleep under canvas

With the starfish

Meet me in the attic

Cobwebs crown your hair

As spiders listen to our strange duet

Open up the battered trunk

Unlock the secrets of one hundred years

Pull back the heavy curtain

Letting in a shaft of light

Dust-fairies dangle

Suspended in dead air

The smell of old books lingers on our skin

Long after we have climbed to the roof

And flown away, hand in hand, towards the moon

Meet me in the graveyard at dead of night

When the clocks strike twelve

Strike a match so I can see your face

Glowing through the black

Mist tethers our ankles to the ground

Below our feet the bodies are as one

Legs become arms

Heads become hearts

And never be lonely again

ABOUT THE AUTHOR

Em Dehaney is a mother of two, a writer of fantasy and a drinker of tea. Born in Gravesend, England, her writing is inspired by the history of her home town. She is made of tea, cake, blood and magic.

By night she is The Black Nun, editor and whip-cracker at Burdizzo Books. By day you can always find her at http://www.emdehaney.com/ or lurking about on Facebook posting pictures of witches https://www.facebook.com/emdehaney/

Her main literary influences are Stephen King, Neil Gaiman, Graham Masterton, H.P. Lovecraft and Poppy Z Brite, and while her published works to date have been mostly horror, Em writes anything that takes her fancy and doesn't like to be pinned down to one genre. A lifelong music lover, Em will listen to everything from acid house to experimental jazz, but her musical inspiration tends to come from Bjork, Fiona Apple, Regina Spektor, PJ Harvey and Super Furry Animals. Her obsessions include reading about Jack The Ripper, Reese's Peanut Butter Cups and smashing the patriarchy.

'Here We Come A-Wassailing', Em's evil folk poem, taken from the Burdizzo Books 12Days Christmas anthology, is to be released as an illustrated mini-book later in 2018. The Burdizzo Books 12Days 2017 contains her vicious short story 'Five Gold Rings'.

Em's most recent Burdizzo release, as both editor and author, is Sparks. Her story The Rape of Ivy House is one of 15 electrifying tales of horror, sci-fi, bizarro and fantasy.

"The brilliance in a book of short stories is never knowing what you'll be getting, even with single-author collections, and SPARKS has a pretty decent selection indeed. From the modern and futuristic, to the daemonic and surreal, the stories on offer here are a fine mix of genres and tastes.

The Rape of Ivy House in particular reminding me of early episodes of Tales of the Unexpected (in the best possible way)."

Paul, Amazon Reviewer

"How do they do it? Here's another amazing anthology from the Burdizzo imprint that's well up to the standard of the previous ones. As before there's a mixture of well-established authors from the Burdizzo stable (Christopher Law and Matthew Cash on cracking form) as well as some that are new to me that I shall look out for in future.

A clever and enjoyable mix of fantasy, whimsy and outright horror."

Haydn Seek, Amazon reviewer

"Only read this when you are alone and in the daylight with clear skies around. The risks are greater if you read during a storm. I extend a round of terrifying applause to Burdizzo Books for giving us one of the best anthologies of the year."

DSJM Reviews

BRAVE BOY
BOOKS

Published in Great Britain by Brave Boy Books 2018

Printed in Great Britain
by Amazon